The Sleepover Club

*Have you been
invited to all these
sleepovers?*

Sleepover Club 2000

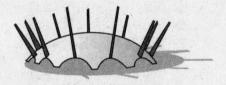

by Angie Bates

Collins

An Imprint of HarperCollins*Publishers*

The Sleepover Club ® is a
registered trademark of HarperCollins*Publishers* Ltd

First published in Great Britain by Collins in 2000
Collins is an imprint of HarperCollins*Publishers* Ltd
77-85 Fulham Palace Road, Hammersmith,
London, W6 8JB

The HarperCollins website address is
www.**fire**and**water**.com

1 3 5 7 9 8 6 4 2

Text copyright © Angie Bates 2000

Original series characters, plotlines
and settings © Rose Impey 1997

ISBN 0 00675488-0

Printed and bound in Great Britain by
Caledonian International Book Manufacturing Ltd,
Glasgow G64

Sleepover Kit List

1. Sleeping bag
2. Pillow
3. Pyjamas or a nightdress
4. Slippers
5. Toothbrush, toothpaste, soap etc
6. Towel
7. Teddy
8. A creepy story
9. Food for a midnight feast:
   chocolate, crisps, sweets, biscuits.
   In fact anything you like to eat.
10. Torch
11. Hairbrush
12. Hair things like a bobble or hairband,
    if you need them
13. Clean knickers and socks
14. Change of clothes for the next day
15. Sleepover diary and membership card

CHAPTER ONE

Oops – sorry! Didn't hurt you, did I? I didn't see you coming round the corner.

These snowflakes glue themselves to your eyelashes. They make everything look dead blurred. Also, don't laugh, but I was kind of pretending I was looking through a veil. You know, a snowy white bride's veil?

Frankie says I've got weddings on the brain, since Mum and Andy announced their engagement. "That's a joke," I told her. "Coming from Miss Frankie 'I've-got-a-new-baby-sister' Thomas!"

It's true. Ever since her baby sister was born, Frankie hasn't stopped rabbiting on about her. Mind you, she *is* the cutest thing. Frankie says she coos in her crib just like a sweet little pigeon!

Look, I'm just on my way to meet Frankie and the others in the school playground. Yes, I *do* know it's Sunday! It's for a really special occasion. And I can't wait to tell you all about it.

Why don't you come with me? That way I can update you on our latest, most radical sleepover yet: Sleepover 2000. (I can't believe I'm saying that, can you?!)

Seriously, I'm quite chilled about the millennium now. But for the first few days, I was truly spooked. I just couldn't picture myself actually living in the year 2000. I mean, that's practically the FUTURE!

Don't tell the others, OK, but when I went to bed on New Year's Eve, I was seriously scared I'd wake up and see alien spaceships buzzing over the rooftops.

But next morning, when I looked out of my

window, there was good old Cuddington, looking disappointingly average! And gradually my millennium worries died down.

At least, they did until I found out where Sleepover 2000 was going to be held. That's right. MY house!

I couldn't *believe* my bad luck. I mean, the first sleepover of the new millennium has got to be truly *awesome*. Everyone's going to remember it for ever and ever. And that's a mega responsibility for anyone, right?

Only with a mum like mine, it's more of a mega *impossibility*.

Don't get me wrong. Mum's the best. But when she was little, she didn't really have that many friends. So every time my mates come round, she goes right over the top trying to make them feel at home. She tries so hard, it gets me all churned up inside.

Plus, a nice home means a lot to Mum. So she's always in a flap in case someone spills their Coke or drops crumbs or whatever.

Unfortunately, at New Year, Mum went just a teeny bit too far. What with the party and her engagement and everything, she was totally stressed out. Then Frankie's mum went into labour, right in the middle of MY mum's party!!! The thought of someone having a baby on her nice new carpet practically sent Mum into orbit.

So you can imagine how I felt about hosting the most important sleepover in history, with Mum fluffing around us the whole time.

I worked myself into a major froth. What made it worse was that there was no-one I could talk to. I couldn't tell the others. They think my mum's a headcase as it is. And I *definitely* couldn't tell Mum.

Then Andy, my soon-to-be-proper stepdad, found me having a cry on the stairs. I told him I didn't feel well. "I think I'm going down with this, like, evil millennium bug everyone's been on about," I sniffled.

But Andy is such a star. After he finally winkled the truth out of me, he totally put my mind at rest. "I'll have a tactful word. Don't give it a second thought, princess," he promised. "Sleepover 2000 is sorted, OK!"

And he gave me a huge clean tissue, so I could give my nose a proper blow.

Mind you, when the Big Day came, it looked like old Andy had let me down. Because—

Oops! There I go again, rushing ahead of myself. I'm such a butterfly. I almost left out the most important part of the story. Which is what happened on our first day back at school.

Have you noticed how bad things mostly happen when you're in a great mood? I mean, not only had I finally got over my sleepover jitters, but I was feeling really bubbly and excited. All five of us were.

And then Mrs Weaver had to go and put a total hex on our plans!!!

CHAPTER TWO

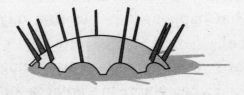

I know this sounds sad, but I was really relieved when it was time to go back to school. After our decorations come down, the Christmas holidays always seem to run out of steam. Mum and I end up watching daft TV programmes about what to do with those unwanted gifts.

Actually, we could have used some tips on *wanted* gifts. Andy was driving us up the wall with the fancy new digital camcorder Mum got him. Mum complained that she couldn't sneeze without him recording it on tape! So with one thing and another, I was quite looking forward to getting back to normal school routine.

You'll never guess what Frankie was talking about when I walked into the classroom. Oh, you guessed!! It turned out her new baby sister still didn't have a name.

"Isn't that really bad luck?" I said.

Frankie scowled. "Not nearly such bad luck as those gross names Mum keeps coming up with. I mean, *Angelica*! Perlease!"

"Is your mum a *Rugrats* fan?" giggled Lyndz.

"Well, that's nothing," said Frankie dramatically. "Wait till you hear Dad's top favourite." She mimed being sick. "EMILY!" she choked.

The five of us went into a collective shudder. Actually, Emily is a really sweet name. Unfortunately, it's also the name of one of the Sleepover Club's biggest enemies, Emily Berryman.

She and Emma Hughes go around in this, like, *deadly* duo. For obvious reasons, we call them the M&Ms. They're always plotting against us.

Just then we had to go into assembly. Every time I looked up, there were the M&Ms, sneaking poisonous little glances at us. They looked exactly like those Siamese cats in *The Lady and the Tramp*!

But after a while I forgot about them. Because 1) Ryan Scott flashed me this really cute smile!! Honestly, he is *such* a dish – and 2) Believe it or not, assembly got really interesting!!!

Mrs Poole had found an old photograph someone had taken of Cuddington villagers at the beginning of the nineteenth century. She'd had a poster-sized blow-up made of it, to show everyone.

Well, OK, if it's not your village, it probably isn't that exciting. But there was something dead touching about seeing all those long-ago villagers in some long-ago Leicestershire meadow. I think the photographer must have interrupted them in the middle of a picnic.

You could just make out one of those really old-fashioned jugs, which Mrs Poole said probably held local cider. You could also see part of a checked tablecloth, half a loaf of bread, and a lump of pork pie.

The photographer had arranged everyone in rows. Grown-ups at the back. Kids at the front. All of them had poker-stiff backs and grim expressions. Even the babies looked stern under their little frilly bonnets!

Mrs Poole explained that in those days, hardly anyone owned a camera.

"This is a tremendously big deal for them. It isn't like some holiday snap you throw away. The photographer is capturing a moment of real history."

I expect you've guessed that our headmistress was leading up to a really big announcement. Isn't it funny how you can tell? It turned out the Parish Council had arranged to have a special millennial photograph taken of today's Cuddingtonians in our school playground!

"So I hope you'll all come along on the last Sunday in January to take *your* place in history," Mrs Poole wound up.

When we got out into the corridor,

everyone was buzzing, discussing what we'd wear for the photograph, so future generations would realise how cool we were.

"It's got to be my Leicester City scarf," said Kenny promptly.

Lyndz giggled. "Oooh, won't you be really cold?"

"I'm wearing my silver jacket. No question," said Frankie. She has this weird thing about silver. I'm surprised she doesn't wear silver knickers.

"I don't know what I'll wear," moaned Rosie.

Me neither. It dawned on me, that I didn't have anything in my whole wardrobe you could truly call *millennial*.

Yippee! Time to go shopping, I thought.

We'd only been back in our class about five minutes when Mrs Weaver brought us down to earth with a bump.

But first I ought to explain that before we broke up for the Christmas holidays, we'd been given a special assignment. We were MEANT to get together with our group over the holidays and brainstorm ideas for what to put in this kind of home-grown Millennium Dome our school was planning.

Well, we'd done the getting together part! Several times. But what with new babies, parties and future weddings, we kind of forgot the homework part.

Everyone else in our class started pulling out long lists and spidergrams and balsa-wood models and I don't know what.

The M&Ms had put together this really slick presentation. They actually gave a TALK to the whole class without Mrs Weaver asking them to! How creepy is *that*!!!

One of them had obviously got a whizzy new computer for Christmas, because they'd printed off this, like, *mega* posh document, listing the most important points in their talk in case we forgot them. Then they strutted round the class, making a big hairy deal out of handing everyone their personal copy. "That way we can have a proper class discussion," smirked Emma, sounding about forty-five years old.

"Yeah, right!" muttered Frankie.

I sat on my hands, wishing the floor would open up and swallow me. The others looked vaguely round the room. Well, except Kenny. She was busy making a paper aeroplane out of you know what!

Actually, I don't think Mrs Weaver had a very nice Christmas. Because when she realised we hadn't done our homework, she went into a total Cruella DeVil act.

"You'll never get anywhere with this kind of sloppy attitude!" she fumed. "Everyone else in this class did as I asked. As a result, they have all earned the right to work on their favourite zones. But you girls will have to put up with whatever is left over!"

Can you guess what "whatever" turned out to be?

Ecology.

But if we thought *this* was bad, Mrs Weaver's next words totally sent us into shock.

"I'm giving you one final chance," she said. "But if you girls don't come up with some really inspiring ideas for your zone by next Monday, you'll be VERY sorry indeed."

We stared at her, like Dalmatian puppies about to be turned into fur coats. We couldn't believe our ears. That meant we'd have to spend our sacred sleepover weekend doing homework!

The M&Ms were loving every minute of it. They could afford to. All their sucking-up totally paid off. They'd landed the all-time coolest zone – the Media Zone. See what I mean? Those girls come up smelling of roses every time!

It was a really horrible morning. And it got even worse. At break time, Mrs Weaver made us all go outside, even though it was cold enough to freeze your eyeballs. We huddled together miserably in our usual corner of the playground and Kenny shared out some Cheesy Wotsits.

Lyndz looked a bit puzzled. "Why are we so upset?" she asked at last. "I thought ecology was a good thing. I mean, it's about saving the planet, isn't it?"

"Yeah, yeah. Ecology is cool and fab and totally groovy," snarled Kenny. "That's why everyone else was falling over themselves to do it."

She glared at the sky, which was filling rapidly with dirty yellow clouds. "Great! It's going to snow," she moaned.

My heart sank. Snow after Christmas has absolutely no point and should be banned.

Frankie collapsed dramatically against the wall. She pulls that kind of stunt all the time. She tells us she's practising for when she's a world-famous actress.

"This sleepover is doomed for ever," she groaned. "I mean, ecology is about recycling, right? Cans and old newspapers and stuff? How depressing is THAT?"

Kenny cheered up. "Hey! We could do something about blood and guts. That's ecology too."

Rosie gulped. "For vampires maybe," she said.

"I thought ecology was, like, mud and Nature," I said.

The others gave me really funny looks.

I hate it when they do that. It makes me feel totally stupid.

"OK, so what are those things, then?" I said sulkily. "You know, those tiny invisible things that live in mud?"

Kenny giggled. "Fliss, you're such a wally! Like we're not in enough trouble. And now you want us to fill an entire zone with invisible mud creatures!"

Everyone cracked up. Including me, I have to admit. Kenny's such a laugh. And I bet you can guess what happened next, can't you? That's right!

Before you could say "hiccups", Lyndz was hiccuping away like a fruit machine. Lyndz is *always* getting hiccups. She drives us crazy.

We started thumping her on the back. "It's OK. They'll go off, hic, in a minute," she gasped. "Look, why can't we do something about, hic, horses?" Lyndz is totally nuts about horses.

"Animals only count if they're endangered," said Kenny in a snooty voice.

"I can't believe Mrs Weaver actually expects us to sacrifice our sleepover for *ecology*," Frankie wailed. "I mean, ecology is so-o *sad*."

"Not as sad as we'll look if we don't come up with something good by Monday," Rosie pointed out.

"Yeah," agreed Lyndz. "The, hic, honour of the entire Sleepover Club is at, hic, hic, stake."

At this point I noticed a tiny flake of snow come circling down. Then another. And another. For some reason those little lonely snowflakes made me feel really helpless.

Frankie was right. Our sleepover was doomed.

I don't feel very well, I thought. In fact, now I came to think about it, my skin felt funny. Hot and kind of sore. My head hurt too.

Well, if that doesn't put the king in the cake, I thought miserably. I'm getting that bug after all. That evil millennium flu bug.

CHAPTER THREE

The first week of term was totally depressing. It didn't even SNOW properly. There was just this really biting wind. And sometimes sleet battered our classroom windows. But on Friday morning, it finally snowed its little socks off!

By lunchtime all the school dustbins had acquired tall frothy hats. Frankie said they looked like giant cappuccinos.

In the afternoon, Mrs Weaver let us skive off to the school library, supposedly to do research for our Ecology Zone. We were still gloomily opening books and shutting them again when Mrs Poole sent a message round, saying the school was closing early because of the bad weather.

"Excellent," said Frankie. "Hope it snows next week too. Then I'll get to see my baby sister loads." Her face lit up. "Did I tell you how she—"

"YES!" we yelled.

"Ssh!" hissed Miss Malone. "This is a library, not a circus!"

"Like we hadn't noticed," muttered Rosie.

"Isn't it weird," said Kenny thoughtfully. "I hate snow, but I *lurve* getting snowed in."

"Me too," said Lyndz. "Don't you love it when they do that Snow Line, and the radio presenter reads out the names of all the schools which are closed, and you hear the magic words 'Cuddington School'?"

"Yeah! And look at it this way," said Rosie. "This means we get a longer sleepover. If it's all right with your mum, Fliss," she added awkwardly.

I crossed my fingers behind my back. "Oh, Mum won't mind," I swanked.

"Great," moaned Frankie. "An extra hour's brain-ache, reading our exciting ecology books. *NOT!*"

The school library was just about to close, so we each grabbed a book and hoped for the best. Lyndz chose a book on horses (surprise, surprise). Kenny found one about the human body, which she said looked "promising". "Gory" is the word I'd use. Kenny wants to be a doctor like her dad. She gets a real kick out of going into disgusting medical details and watching her friends squirm! My book showed all the weird little things you can see in an ordinary rain puddle. Well, if you've got a microscope! I was going to prove the existence of my mysterious mud creatures if it *killed* me.

I hate going out in ice and snow, don't you? It makes me dead nervous and wobbly, like I'm going to fall on my face and knock my teeth out. And as I tottered down our road, a whole hour earlier than usual, I started feeling wobbly on the inside too.

Suppose Andy's "tactful word" only made

things worse? Mum's dead sensitive. You can't predict what's going to set her off.

"Please don't let her embarrass me in front of my friends," I prayed. "I'll never ask for another thing."

But when I turned my key, Mum was on the other side of the door with a big grin on her face. I could see she was bursting to tell me something.

"Is it OK if everyone comes early, Mum?" I asked.

She nodded brightly. "Everything's been ready for hours."

My tummy turned over. "Ready?" I stuttered. "But Andy—?"

Mum's expression went all soft and gooey. "Bless him. He was so sweet. He explained that he loves me just the way I am, but that me being so house-proud sometimes puts a bit of a strain on you all."

I swallowed. "But—"

"He made me see I've got to learn to be more relaxed," said Mum. "More fun to be with."

"*More* fun?" I said in dismay.

"Anyway, I was wondering what I could do to make this a really extra-special year 2000 sleepover for you all, when I heard this man on the car radio," Mum burbled. "And then I had my brainwave."

"Brainwave?" I echoed. Brainstorm, more like.

Mum wagged her finger. "You're not getting another word out of me until your friends get here. Just keep out of my hair, while I do the finishing touches."

I went upstairs in a daze. It was like a bad dream. Andy's tactful advice had only made my try-hard mum try harder than ever! What *is* she up to down there? I wondered nervously. Redecorating the house?

Just then, I saw the other members of the Sleepover Club out of the window, happily galumphing into view.

Boy, I had to move FAST! I raced down the stairs two at a time, and got the door open a split second before Frankie leaned on the door chimes.

"There's a problem," I gasped. "You see, my mum—"

"Don't worry," grinned Rosie. "Boots off already. Look!" She wiggled her toes in their woolly socks.

"And mine *nearly* are," said Lyndz, hopping on one foot. "Don't worry. Your mum's carpets are safe with us."

"We'll leave our coats in the porch," said Kenny, "so they won't drip where they shouldn't."

"You don't understand!" I wailed. "It isn't a carpet-type problem. It's more of a total—"

I was going to say "disaster". But before I could warn my friends they were about to be zapped by my mother's extra-special year 2000 brainwave, Mum appeared.

"Hi everyone," she sang. "Great to see you all! I wonder if you'd just mind putting all those snowy boots and coats back on and coming round to the *back* of the house instead?"

Everyone's mouths fell open. No-one said a word. But I knew what they were thinking.

I was thinking the exact same thing. My mum had *totally* lost the plot!

Carefully not meeting my eye, Frankie and the others put their snowy boots and coats back on, and squelched out of our front porch without a word.

"Go with them, Fliss. That bolt on the back gate is a bit tricky," said Mum. Honestly, she was beaming so brightly you could have used her for a Belisha beacon.

I threw on my coat and crunched after them, wondering if it was possible for a person to die of shame.

One of our neighbours had a bonfire going. I could smell smoke and something I couldn't quite put a name to.

I unbolted the back gate, and wouldn't you know? I managed to pinch my finger. It *really* hurt. Great, that's all I need, I thought – a thumping great blood blister. I held the gate open with one hand and sucked the other hand miserably. Everyone trudged past into our sparkling white garden.

But as they disappeared round the corner, I heard gasps of astonishment.

"*Coo-ell!*" shouted Lyndz.

"Hey, Fliss!" yelled Kenny. "What a wicked surprise!"

I followed them. It was a surprise all right.

Fairy lights twinkled on the snowy patio. Wispy blue smoke rose into the evening air.

The barbecue, I thought in a daze. *That*'s what I could smell. It had reached exactly the right red-hot stage for cooking too – something Mum doesn't always get right. Foil-wrapped goodies were roasting on the bars, alongside sizzling sausages and burgers.

Mum was handing round steaming mugs. "It should be vodka," she teased. "But I thought your parents might not approve."

When Kenny looked up from her mug, she had a blob of cream on her nose. "Heaven," she whispered. "I'm in hot chocolate heaven."

Mum had thought of absolutely *everything*. She'd even set up a big spotty parasol to keep off the snow. The table was laid with cutlery, pretty paper plates, and even *more* goodies.

Mum put her arm round me. "This man on the radio said that in Siberia it's perfectly normal to have winter picnics. So I thought, if the Russians can do it, why can't we?" Her voice trailed off. "You don't *mind* having a picnic in the snow, do you?"

"Mind!" shrieked Kenny. "This is ACE!"

"It's magic!" chortled Rosie.

"Outrageous," agreed Lyndz.

Frankie didn't say a word. She stared around our back garden as if she couldn't believe her eyes. I couldn't tell what she was thinking. But being Frankie, I knew it was bound to be something dead sarky.

Suddenly she started fumbling in her bag. She fished out a canary-yellow camera, one of those funky Polaroid ones.

"Mrs Sidebotham," she said, in her most polite voice. "Would you take a picture of us, please? I want to remember this awesome sleepover my whole life!"

CHAPTER FOUR

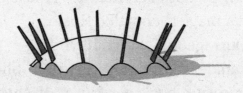

When I was little, every time I got the teensiest bit excited about anything, Granny Sidebotham (that's my real dad's mum) used to say, "Mark my words. There'll be tears before bedtime."

What a thing to say to a little kid! Like, "Don't ever have fun, Felicity, or something bad will happen!"

Well, it's a good thing Gran wasn't invited to our snow picnic, because, not counting Christmas, it has to be the MOST fun I ever had in winter!

We stuffed our faces till our buttons practically popped off. But even after the food was gone, our fairy-lit garden felt so incredibly magic, no-one could bear to go back indoors.

It had practically stopped snowing by this time. Just an occasional, totally perfect snowflake drifted down. Lyndz stuck out her tongue and tasted one. "I wish we could stay out here all night," she said.

"Andy would have to thaw us with his blowtorch in the morning," I shivered.

The temperature was so far below zero by this time, Mum's picnicking Siberians would have been completely at home.

Suddenly Kenny had the bright idea of putting on all the clothes she'd brought with her! We all rushed inside, and soon we were all throwing on every garment we could find. It was like that dressing up-race we had on Sports Day in the Infants. (Which I always lost, incidentally. Not because I was bad at sports. I was ace, thanks very much! More because I was the only kid who took the dressing-up part really seriously!)

I think Mum still felt bad about her New Year freak-out, because she kept herself totally under control while we piled on the layers, even though it meant us dripping melted snow all over her clean kitchen floor.

"That's better," sighed Lyndz, when we were back outside. "Nice and toasty again."

The only problem was that all the extra clothes made our arms totally stick out at the sides. We were all moving dead stiffly.

"We look like robots," Lyndz giggled.

"Or Teletubbies," suggested Rosie. And she went into this hysterical Teletubby impersonation. Soon we were all waddling about, talking in silly baby voices like Tinky Winky and La La and whatever.

"Hey, we can be the Snowtubbies," I said suddenly.

This made Lyndz laugh so hard she had a complete choking fit, which probably makes her the only hiccupping Snowtubby in history. Mind you, her hiccups stopped in record time when Kenny threatened to stuff a big handful of snow down her neck! Now all we had to do was get Lyndz out of her major sulk! Eventually Rosie persuaded her to make snow angels with us.

Oh, if you're interested in having a go, here's the Sleepover Club's Three-Step Guide to snow-angel making!

FIRST, you fall backwards gracefully into a snowdrift, OK? Oh, yeah! TOP TIP. Pick a patch of snow without a prickly bush underneath. Frankie didn't. So her first attempt wasn't as graceful as it could have been. It also hurt a LOT!!!

SECOND, kind of wiggle your arms and feet about in the snow.

THIRD, jump up again, and prepare to be amazed by the really cool and creative angel print you have left behind!!

Except ours weren't, really. Cool, I mean. Owing to those woolly extra layers, our angels were more like Snowtubbies with wings! When Mum saw them, she laughed till she cried!

Mum was still being a total star. While we were Snowtubbying about, she got busy making a whole new batch of barbecue goodies. All the yummy things she doesn't normally let me eat. Toasted marshmallows. Bananas in foil with melty hot chocolate inside.

"This is all terribly fattening," Mum said apologetically as she handed them round.

"Who cares!" said Frankie stickily.

"It's only once in a millennium," mumbled Kenny, through a mouthful of hot marshmallow.

"That's what I thought," said Mum. And lightning-quick, she snaffled a piece of deliciously squidgy banana and popped it in her mouth! She licked her fingers and gave a naughty grin. I couldn't believe my eyes. Mum is a *total* diet fanatic.

"Want to go indoors yet?" I asked the others hopefully. I was getting *incredibly* cold, but I wasn't going to be the first person to wimp out!

But Rosie said no-one was allowed back in the house until we'd built a Sleepover Club snowman.

"She's right," sighed Kenny. "It's gotta be done, guys."

Lyndz didn't look too keen either. "OK," she said. "But let's set a deadline. Like we've got to make this snowman in ten minutes or something!"

"Wicked!" said Frankie at once. "The Funky Ten-Minute Snowman. But first we've got to get him all his snowman necessities."

"Like a face," spluttered Rosie, totally falling about at her own joke. We all cracked up.

"Imagine my poor little brother waking up in the dark and seeing a snowman without a face," I giggled. "He'd have a total fit."

Frankie did her croaky film-trailer voice. "Just when you thought it was safe to play in the snow, little boy!"

"I'm walking in the air," sang Kenny. "With no eyeballs or hair!"

"Or thermal underwear!" shrieked Frankie.

I could see Mum thinking it was a really good thing she'd taken Callum round to Dad and Maria's. Oh, Maria's my dad's girlfriend –

they just live round the corner with my little half-sister Posy. Also, Maria's got her own little boy, Martin. Me and Callum go round there all the time. I'm so lucky, having *two* really great dads.

Sorry, I lost the plot there for a minute! I was going to tell you what we collected for our Ten-Minute Snowman Kit. OK, here goes:

Pebbles for eyes, of course. (We had to scrabble in the snow for those.) Plus a cork nose and a toothy orange-peel grin. Oh, and some of those fogey old buttons which look like miniature half-footballs. Mum gave us a tatty scarf and this gruesome old cap which Andy *lurves* to wear at weekends (she'd been trying to prise it off him for ages!). Then Mum set the oven pinger, and off we went.

Ever tried building a snowman to a tight deadline? Honestly, it was *such* a laugh! For one thing, our fingers were so numb we had almost NO control over them. Kenny said it was like trying to pick up sweets with those totally impossible little cranes you get at funfairs.

I think it dawned on us, at almost exactly the same moment, that there was no WAY this snowman was going to be finished by the time the pinger went off.

Lyndz pulled a disgusted face. "This snowman looks so-o stoopid," she sighed.

"Too geeky for words," agreed Frankie.

"If you ask me, he needs a serious make-over," smirked Rosie.

"Absolutely," said Kenny. And just a second too late, I saw the gleam in her eye.

Suddenly a handful of snowman came whizzing through the air and whacked me on the side of the head. "Hey!" I said.

And all at once I was in the middle of a wild snowball fight. OK, snow*man* fight, if you want to be picky. Soon there was so much snowman wreckage flying around, the garden looked like it had been hit by a major blizzard.

I think we must have been making a lot of noise, because our grumpy next-door neighbour, Mrs Watson-Wade, looked out of her upstairs window and made this, like, mega production out of drawing the curtains.

Then suddenly the party was over. We were all tired out.

It felt dead peculiar being back indoors. Too stuffy and MUCH too bright. We hopped around in our socks, blinking like owls, trying to rub warmth back into our hands and feet.

"Why does thawing out hurt so much?" Rosie whimpered.

Mum brought us fluffy towels so we could dry ourselves off. Then she made more hot drinks. I was mentally awarding her Brownie points for being such a cool mum, when Frankie caught sight of our kitchen clock. Her expression totally clouded over.

"Is that the time?" she gasped. "We'll *never* get that stupid project done now! We'll probably have to stay up all night!"

The party sparkle went out of Mum's eyes. "You didn't tell me you had homework, Fliss," she said.

"We haven't really," I fibbed.

"Yeah, *right*. We've only got to plan an entire Ecology Zone by Monday," said Frankie in a snappish voice. "And we've only like, totally wasted hours and hours!"

"Frankie!" everyone hissed.

But it was too late. Mum looked incredibly hurt.

Suddenly Frankie burst into tears. "It's all right for you lot," she bawled. "It's not *your* sister who's going to have her life ruined on the stroke of midnight!"

Huh? Honestly, that girl is such a drama queen!

Everyone stared at her in total confusion.

"What *are* you on about?" said Kenny.

"That's their final deadline. Midnight tonight. If Mum and Dad can't agree on a name by then, they're just going to pull one out of a hat. My little sister will be stuck with it for ever and ever."

Mum handed her the tissue box. Frankie took one and wiped her eyes. "Heaven knows what they'll come up with," she wept. "Without me there to keep an eye on things.

I mean what if they call her something so pathetic that all the other little kids make fun of her?"

Like me being called Sidebotham, I thought. I didn't say this aloud though, because Mum would have been really upset. Anyway, it was strictly first names we were discussing here.

"They named *you* OK," Kenny pointed out. "I don't know what you're so worried about."

"Then I'll tell you what I'm so worried about," said Frankie, working herself into a real Frankie-type froth. "I'm worried because I absolutely know what my little sister should be called, OK? I've come up with the PERFECT name, OK? But when it comes to really important decisions, big sisters don't seem to count for some reason. Of course, if my parents want something boring doing, that's totally different. 'Frankie, sweetheart, warm this bottle up!' 'Frankie, be a love and fetch the talcum powder!' 'Frankie—'"

"Why don't you phone home now?" Mum suggested quickly. "Ask your parents if they'd let you put *your* choice into the hat along with theirs."

Frankie blinked in surprise. "Really?" she said. "Do you think they would?"

Mum shrugged. "What have you got to lose? Hold on, I'll get you the phone."

Frankie dived into the hall with our portable phone and shut the door. I could hear a tiny electronic beep each time she pushed a button. She was in such a state she kept getting wrong numbers.

The others looked totally embarrassed. I wasn't. I was steaming mad. I know my mum isn't the most relaxed person on this planet, but she'd tried really hard to give everyone a good time, and Frankie had been dead disrespectful. Huh! I thought. I bet it never even *occurs* to that girl to say sorry!

Kenny cleared her throat. "I thought Frankie was crazy about her baby sister," she whispered.

"Being a big sister takes getting used to, bird-brain," hissed Lyndz. "I felt the same when my little brother was born."

So did I. But I couldn't very well say so, with Mum earwigging about two inches away.

Unfortunately, Frankie came back in a worse mood than ever.

"I got our stupid answer service," she moaned. "I had to leave a message, which my parents will probably be too busy to pick up." Then she looked a bit ashamed. "Oh, thanks for the phone, Mrs Sidebotham," she mumbled.

"OK," sighed Lyndz. "Enough. Get out your books."

She zonked her horse book down on our dining-room table with a mighty crash. I could feel Mum *forcing* herself not to check if Lyndz had made a big scratch or not. And my old mixed-up feelings came churning back.

Rosie blew her hair out of her eyes. "This is *so-o* hopeless!" she said. "We're in doom forever."

"Doom city," agreed Frankie.

"How come you guys are so freaked out by

44

some stupid little word?" said Kenny in disgust. "Ecology is no big deal, honestly. I asked Dad about it and we looked it up together. It just means how everything in nature is all connected and, like, WORKS together."

We stared at her blankly.

"Well, you soon changed your tune, Laura McKenzie," growled Frankie.

Kenny shrugged. "Dad says we've just got to find an angle. A way to make ecology fun."

"Yeah, right," said Frankie. "Ecology is fun. Why didn't I think of that?"

Kenny and Frankie glared at each other. There was a kind of awkward silence. Then Frankie slammed her book shut.

"This is a total waste of time!" she yelled.

Unfortunately, she must have caught her drink with her elbow at the same time.

Oh-oh. One of Mum's best mugs went crashing to the floor in a kind of spooky slow motion. We watched helplessly. It was like we were so horrified, no-one could move a muscle.

Frankie stared at the mess as if she had no idea how it got there.

Mum came zooming to the rescue. "No use crying over spilled milk, you guys," she babbled bravely. "These things happen."

She sounded exactly like Granny Sidebotham trying to be cool and groovy. And this made ME so upset that for some reason I grabbed the Vanish right out of her hand. "Just stop fussing, Mum," I yelled. "*I'll* do it, OK!"

Which was incredibly mean of me. Because Mum felt quite bad enough, thank you very much. Her Siberian picnic had got our year 2000 sleepover off to a brilliant start. Too brilliant, obviously. Because now the whole operation had crashed and burned.

There were going to be tears before bedtime, just like Gran always said. And neither Mum nor I knew what to do about it.

CHAPTER FIVE

We trawled gloomily through our books for inspiration. Then we all sighed heavily, swapped over and tried again.

There were some interesting rude diagrams in Kenny's. But otherwise we came up with a big fat ZERO.

Mum was fluffing about again, totally getting on my nerves. She kept whisking our mugs away before we'd actually finished our drinks, and pulling back the dining-room curtains and closing them again.

"*Mum*," I said. "We're trying to think, OK?"

"Sorry," she said. "It's just that Andy's not usually this late. And with this weather..." Her voice trailed away.

I stared at her. I'd completely failed to notice Andy hadn't come home. "Did you ring his mobile?"

She shook her head.

"Ring it now," I said.

Mum wrung her hands. "I'm probably being silly."

Neither of us could bring ourselves even to whisper the word "accident".

At that moment the back door opened, letting in gusts of freezing air. Andy stood in the doorway, stamping snow off his shoes.

I'll never understand grown-ups. You'd think Mum would be really pleased to see him. Instead, she nearly bit his head off.

"Where have you been?" she snapped. "I've been out of my mind!"

"Sorry, love," said Andy. "At one point I thought I was going to have to leave the car on the other side of Cuddington and walk."

Mum's eyes widened. "Are you OK? Is the car OK?"

Andy hugged her. "The car and I are both fine. I didn't have an accident, if that's what you're thinking." He grinned at me. "A little bit of snow and your mum's got me dead and buried. Oh, and the answer's 'yes', Nikki," he teased. "A nice cup of tea would be just the job after that long cold drive, thanks for asking."

Mum rushed around, fetching Andy dry socks and hot drinks and boosting the thermostat to totally tropical levels.

I rolled my eyes at the others. "Sorry," I mouthed.

Andy joined us at the table. "How's it going, girls?" he said.

He was just being friendly, but now I knew he wasn't dead, I wanted him to go away and stay out of our hair.

I glared. "Actually we're busy," I said.

As you've probably guessed, it takes more than a glare to embarrass Andy Proudlove. Yes, that IS his full name. And guess what?

After the wedding, it's going to be mine as well. How come I get lumbered with two totally STOO-PID, totally humiliating names?

Anyway, Andy started chatting away about this protest demo he'd run into on his way home. Apparently, protesters were stopping drivers to explain what their demo was about.

Instead of being fed up with them for getting between him and his tea, Andy sounded impressed. "Say what you like, they've got some bottle camping out in this weather. It's enough to freeze your—"

"Do you *mind*," I moaned. "We've got this project."

Mum sat down too. "It must have been a big protest to make you this late." And she cosied up to Andy.

Andy put his cold hand over hers. Mum shrieked and pushed him away. "You're not kidding," he grinned. "They caused a serious traffic jam. They were better than the circus. Flaming torches, banners, painted faces."

"What were they demonstrating about?" asked Mum.

Who CARES! I screamed silently. Couldn't my parents see they were totally ruining my life, just by *being* there?!

I tried beaming deadly thought-rays. But Andy was immune to them too. He went warbling on about how someone was building some massive DIY outlet near our village.

"I heard about that!" said Kenny suddenly. She sounded interested. "Mum says it's a disgrace to even think of building on Browses Piece."

"Browses Piece?" said Rosie. "I don't think I've been there."

"Me neither," I yawned. "Shouldn't we get back to this—"

"Yes you have, bird-brain," Lyndz interrupted. "You've been *loads* of times. It's on the way to Leicester," she explained to Rosie. "I go riding near there. There's a little turn-off, right? You go down a little twisty lane and there it is. In spring and summer it's totally gorgeous."

"OK," I said. "I do remember. Now let's get on with this project."

But they totally ignored me.

"I just *lurve* that place," gushed Frankie. "Mum used to take me when I was a little kid. She's got this picture of me, toddling around in the flowers. I'm so small, it looks like I'm in a daisy and buttercup jungle!"

"If you believe these protesters, our village is about to lose a piece of paradise," Andy wittered on. "Not just primroses and whatnot. But all kinds of wildlife apparently."

How come Andy was suddenly so keen on Nature? Mum can't usually drag him away from the snooker long enough to cut our grass!

Frankie gave a gasp. "Nobody move!" she said.

"It's not a spider, is it?" quavered Mum.

Frankie had an incredibly tense expression, like someone waiting for a sneeze. "I have had the most AWESOME idea," she announced.

Honestly, that girl! Of course, she'd got everyone staring at her now.

"Remember the photograph Mrs Poole

showed us, of those villagers at the beginning of the nineteenth century? Well, where do you think it was taken?" She waited for us to catch on.

Lyndz looked puzzled. "Browses Piece, wasn't it?"

"Yeah, definitely," said Kenny.

Frankie beamed around the room. "Isn't that a totally incredible coincidence?"

Everyone looked blank.

"Don't you see how perfect it is?" she said, waving her arms like a windmill. "Here's this lovely little beauty spot which has been here, like, forever. I mean, our grandparents and great-grandparents used to go there to chill out with *their* kids. And now thanks to some horrible DIY company, my baby sister might never set eyes on even ONE of those buttercups. I mean, is this serious ecology or WHAT?"

"So are you saying, forget all the big stuff in the books and do something about Browses Piece instead?" Kenny asked.

Frankie nodded. "Mrs Weaver will love it!"

"Sounds great," said Andy. "Think globally. Act locally."

Mum gave him a funny look.

"I read that on one of their banners," he said bashfully.

Suddenly Kenny slapped Frankie on the back. "Spaceman," she grinned. "You finally cracked the case!"

"Yeah. Nice one, Frankie!" said Lyndz.

"Coo-ell!" agreed Rosie.

I felt like the only person in the soap opera without a script!

"But what would we be DOING exactly?" I said.

Frankie scowled. "I can't have ALL the ideas. The rest of you do some thinking for a change."

"Ooooh!" teased Lyndz. "That's telling you, Fliss!"

"I've got an idea," said Mum. "If you don't mind me butting in?"

Everyone made polite noises.

She looked dead shy. "Well, since you've only got till Monday, why don't I drive you up to the protest site tonight, to take a look around?"

I couldn't believe my ears. "Are you kidding? It's *freezing* out there. All those little side roads will be, like, deadly death-traps!"

"Just a suggestion," said Mum calmly. "I thought you girls might be up for an adventure."

"You can count me in," said Frankie at once.

"And me," said Rosie. "I'll finally get to see Browses Piece."

"Yeah, under three feet of snow," I muttered.

"I think it's a brilliant idea," said Lyndz.

"Totally," agreed Kenny.

It was awful. Everyone seemed really excited. Everyone except me.

"It'll be pitch dark," I wailed.

"We've got torches," said Mum.

How did this happen? Now I'd turned into the worry-wart and Mum was the dare-devil! She'd be wearing motorbike leathers next!!

"What would be cool," said Frankie, in her most actressy voice, "is if we had a *reeeally* good camcorder, so we could, like, interview protesters for our Ecology Zone." And she looked straight at Andy as she said it.

"You're in luck," said Andy. "Nikki got me a fantastic new camcorder for Christmas!"

"How AMAZING!" said Frankie, acting like this was totally news.

"What a shame," I sighed. "Dad will be bringing Callum home any minute now. There's no way we can take him to some freezing cold protest site. Not with his chest."

My little brother catches everything going. Normally Mum totally wraps him up in cotton wool. One–nil to me, I crowed to myself. THAT should do the trick.

Only it didn't.

"No probs, Fliss," said Andy. "One phone call should fix that. Steve and Maria won't mind." He glanced at Mum. "It's only once in a millennium."

If one more person uses that phrase I personally am going to SCREAM, I thought.

Mum went skipping off to organise

Thermos flasks. "Make me a nice fat sandwich while you're at it, Nikki," Andy called. "I'll eat when we come back."

Obviously Andy was inviting himself on this insane expedition too!

The others started pulling on sweaters and socks, chatting away. I put mine on too. I mean, I didn't exactly have a *choice*.

This is what they mean by "Millennium Fever", I thought. People rushing round doing stupid things they'd never usually dream of doing.

Like squandering precious sleepover hours in a cold, dark field, with a bunch of hairy weirdos.

"Cheer up, princess," grinned Andy as we piled into the car. "It may never happen."

I folded my arms across my chest, to show my parents I was totally *not* impressed. "Huh!" I said.

CHAPTER SIX

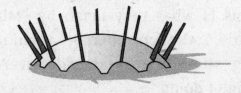

The main road was deserted as we drove out of the village. I decided anyone with any sense was in the warm, watching telly. A huge moon floated over the snowy fields. Isn't it peculiar, the way the moon always seems to be, like, personally following your car?

Mum and Andy were chatting about the wedding. Well, Mum did most of the talking. Andy said stuff like "Mmm" and "Nice one" and "Ouch. That's a bit pricey, Nikki."

Suddenly Kenny gave me a poke in the

ribs. "Aren't you going to stand up to Frankie, you wally?" she growled.

"What?" I said stupidly.

Can you guess what the quarrel was about? Frankie was only telling everyone *she* was going to operate our camcorder! I can't *believe* that girl sometimes.

"The protest was MY idea," Frankie was saying. "If it wasn't for me, the rest of you wouldn't even BE here."

Boy, did Kenny get mad then! "And YOU wouldn't be here if it wasn't for Fliss," she told her. "Look, we're a team, OK? That means we all work together."

"I know what 'team' means, thanks very much," snapped Frankie. "It means we all do the job we're best at. And filming is my thing. Everyone knows that."

"We don't know that at all," I said. "Admit it! You're just peeved because the M&Ms got the Media Zone."

Actually, I think Andy would make an excellent secret agent. Can you believe he was earwigging our back-seat quarrel at the same time he and Mum were having their wedding chat!

"No offence, girls," he chipped in. "But there's no way I'm letting any of you loose with my new camcorder." He sounded friendly but dead firm.

"Oh," said Frankie in a shocked voice. And she totally shut up.

One–nil to Andy, I thought. I could have hugged him. Well, if he wasn't driving.

"But I don't want to be a party pooper," Andy went on. "So how about if Fliss and Frankie share the interviewing, and I tag along as, like, your loyal cameraman?"

Frankie cheered up at once. I told you she fancies herself as a media star.

Personally I hate being videoed. Especially for something that's going to be seen by the whole school. Even if I did the interview hiding behind the camera, you'd still hear my voice. I HATE the sound of my voice on tape. It's so-o weedy. Like a squeaky little gerbil.

"Frankie can do it," I said. "I don't know what to say."

"'Course you don't, princess," said Andy. He flashed me a huge grin. "There isn't anything TO say, yet! This film crew is still in transit!"

He flicked on the indicator and turned into Browses Lane. "Hello," he said. "We've hit a traffic jam."

He was exaggerating. There were four cars crawling along in front of us. The lane hadn't been gritted and was incredibly slippy.

Suddenly the back end of the car began to slide sideways. I heard a scared gerbil squeak coming from somewhere. Then I realised it was me!

Luckily Andy's an excellent driver. He corrected the skid really quickly. "No cause for alarm, girls," he said. "Just checking you're all still awake!"

"If they do build this DIY place," said Mum, as if we hadn't all nearly died in a ditch, "wouldn't they have to build a proper road?"

"The DIY outfit is just the start, if you ask me," said Andy. "Before you know it, they'll sneak in one of those massive supermarkets and I don't know what else."

But I'd stopped listening again. Apart from the moon and the car headlights, it was totally dark. I felt a tingle of excitement.

OK, I'll admit it! I was a tiny bit thrilled to be here. Even if the rest of me wished it was safe at home in the warm.

Suddenly, red and yellow flames kind of sprang out of the dark. My heart gave a big jump inside my chest. Like it was saying, "Yippee! Adventures!" I think the others felt the same, because we all started grinning at each other.

"Ace," said Kenny. "Camp fires."

"This is *such* a radical sleepover," said Lyndz.

"Yeah, Fliss," said Rosie. I felt myself blushing in the dark.

Andy stopped the car. To my surprise, there were loads of cars parked there already.

"Oh-oh, I recognise that Volvo!" Rosie hissed.

Guess what! Andy had parked right next to Mrs Poole's car.

I had a horrible thought. "You don't think

the M&Ms will be here as well, do you?"
I asked the others.

"You *are* kidding," said Kenny. "Coming
here would be WAY too dangerous for them!
I expect they're at home by the fire, knitting
themselves a life."

"Now, now," Andy teased. We were all still
giggling as we piled out of the car.

In case you didn't know, Browses Piece
used to be part of some huge, really ancient
forest. I didn't know myself until recently. To
tell you the truth, it was all just grass and
trees to me. And you don't think of them as
being in *danger*, do you?

Suddenly Rosie froze beside me. "You
didn't tell me Browses Piece was haunted!"
she whispered.

I felt all the tiny hairs stand up on the back
of my neck. Dozens of pale little lights were
flitting around in the dark.

But they weren't ghosts, just live human
beings trying to find their way in the pitch
dark with torches, storm lanterns, even tatty
bits of candle. Now and then, someone

The Sleepover Club

tripped over a guy rope and said something rude. We couldn't believe it. Browses Piece was full of people!

There were tents all over the place. Some of them were dead basic, just bent tree branches covered with heavy-duty polythene. I think they belonged to the serious protesters. It was like *Robin Hood, Prince of Thieves*. Only better, because you could actually smell wood smoke.

Frankie slipped her arm through mine. That's one good thing about her. She never holds grudges very long. "You've got to clock this," she giggled. "They've built these cute little Ewok houses in the wood."

To humour her, I craned my neck and peered into the smoky darkness. Guess what? Frankie wasn't kidding. There were lights high in the branches. Just like that wild tree-top town in *Return of the Jedi*!

Don't laugh, but I thought some of the protesters looked dead unfriendly. Body-piercing doesn't bother me – well, you know, in Leicester city centre, by daylight. But it's

64

different when you're in a field, miles from anywhere.

Every time Andy caught someone in the beam of the torch, there was this totally scary glitter of metal. Honestly, they were like some weird kind of alien. Some of them had shaved most of their hair off. You could see, like, their bare skulls. And I don't just mean the boys!

"Bet you they've got serious tattoos under those big coats," Rosie whispered.

"Are *all* these people protesters?" said Lyndz.

"I think some of them are just well-wishers," said Andy.

"There's Mrs Diggins," said Mum, sounding surprised. And she went over to say hello.

Mr and Mrs Diggins are this sweet old couple Mum has known for ever. Mr Diggins is always in and out of hospital. But his wife is still totally full of beans. In fact, she's a bit outrageous. She does yoga and belly-dancing and all sorts! Also, Mum says she has perfect skin. You know, for an old person.

Mum was waving us over.

"Do we have to?" I moaned to Andy.

Before Mum's interruption, Mrs Diggins had been chatting to some really heavy-duty protesters. Now they were all staring at us.

I felt really out of place. You could tell they were the type of people who would automatically despise a person just because she wore Dizzy Disco Pink nail varnish.

One of the protesters was this, like, bald *giant*, with major body-piercing. After I'd clocked him, I didn't even dare *look* at the others! But Mrs Diggins was totally at home.

"Hello Fliss, dear," she said. "I was just telling Travis that Dan and I did our courting here, over fifty years ago. In fact, this is where Dan asked me to marry him. And ever since then, it's been our special place. So when I heard about this protest, I simply *had* to come. I think you young people are wonderful." She beamed up at the giant.

People can really surprise you sometimes. I mean, Travis can't have chatted to Mrs Diggins longer than five minutes, yet he'd winkled all this really personal information out of her.

Travis turned to me. "Your mum says you want to film us," he said. "For your Millennium project."

I'm such a sad person. When I get nervous, I don't make any sense at all. "Erm, thank you," I said. "Well, actually it's all of us. Also, it's not quite exactly a film—"

Frankie rescued me. "Yes, it is," she said quickly. "And it's going to be mind-blowingly brilliant." She gave a cheeky grin. "Want to be in it?"

"No fear," shuddered Travis. "I go to pieces in front of a camera. Anyway, I've got a better idea."

Without another word, he strode away. Then he looked back. "Come on," he said. "I want you to meet someone."

I tugged Andy's sleeve. "Andy," I said. "Erm..."

He grinned. "I'm right behind you, princess," he said.

And we followed Travis into the dark.

CHAPTER SEVEN

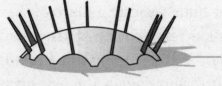

As we followed Travis through the crowd, Andy filmed everything in sight. Boy, Mum went to town when she bought that new camcorder! You can even film in slo-mo. Is that cool or what! And it has a funky little monitor which gives instant play-back. So you don't have to wait until you can get to a video machine.

You're probably wondering what anyone could find to film in a dark field, aren't you?

Well, believe it or not, the protest site was turning out to be unexpectedly interesting. Andy was right. It WAS like the circus!

We saw a fire-eater and stilt walkers, and a girl juggling with brightly coloured clubs – you know, glittery metallic-type ones. They looked dead magic, whizzing around her in the dark. Kenny said they looked like flying fish. I didn't know fish could fly, did you?

All around us there were people chanting and drumming. One protester actually started playing a didgeridoo. I always thought digeridoos were a bit sad, like saying you play the triangle or tambourine or something. But the sound was so incredible it made me break into major goosebumps. The atmosphere was amazing. I really started getting into it. So did Andy.

"Reminds me of Glastonbury Festival," he sighed.

"I never knew you went to Glastonbury," I said.

"Twice," said Andy. "Mind you, I was a young man then."

"Did they have festivals in the olden days?" said Kenny cheekily.

"Sweetheart, we *invented* festivals," Andy told her.

We were getting out of breath. Travis had such long legs, we had to run to keep up. Luckily, he kept stopping and asking people if they'd seen someone called Jewel, which gave us the chance to recover.

"Yo, Pollen! Seen Jewel?" Travis yelled suddenly.

"That's one name your parents never thought of," Kenny whispered to Frankie. "Mmm, Pollen Thomas. I like it!"

Frankie rolled her eyes. "This place is too hippie dippie for words," she muttered.

Anyway Pollen hadn't. Seen Jewel, I mean. Not recently, anyway.

But a few minutes later, a girl caught us up.

"Looking for me, Trav?" she said cheekily.

"These young ladies want to put you in their film," grinned Travis.

Then he strode away without saying goodbye, leaving us staring at each other like lemons.

I won't pretend Jewel exactly fell over herself with excitement when she saw us.

But she didn't look totally hostile either. It was more like she was weighing us up. We were probably staring too, weighing HER up!

Jewel was about our age. She was actually quite pretty, in a scrubbed, freckly sort of way. (Mind you, her hair could have *really* used a good conditioner.) The good news was that Jewel didn't seem to go in for body-piercing. Well, a little nose stud and a few earrings, but nothing weird.

"Aren't you going to tell me your names?" she asked.

We remembered our manners and introduced ourselves, but I think Jewel could tell we felt dead uncomfortable.

"Don't mind me," grinned Andy. "You girls get acquainted."

There was another long silence.

"So, what's this about a film?" Jewel asked.

We all started babbling at once. Then we stopped at the same moment and went into a major fit of the giggles, which Jewel totally joined in.

"Look, why don't you guys come back to the van?" she suggested. "And tell me in comfort."

"That would be great," said Kenny.

"Ace," said Lyndz.

Actually, I wasn't too sure I wanted to go into Jewel's van, to be honest. I know it sounds snobby, but I couldn't see how anyone could POSSIBLY keep themselves clean, living like that.

We trudged across the site to the van Jewel shared with her mum.

The snow was getting really mushed up with so many people around.

"Hope you don't mind," said Jewel, when we arrived. "But Mum has this rule about boots and shoes. We generally leave them inside the door. Otherwise the van turns into a swamp."

"My mum has the same rule," I said.

We cautiously followed Jewel inside.

"Ooh, it's really cosy in here," said Lyndz, sounding surprised.

"Mum's a heat freak," Jewel explained.

72

"She insisted on getting the most powerful wood-burner she could physically fit in our van!"

By this time I think my mouth had actually dropped open.

Jewel's home was GORGEOUS!

I mean, it was quite untidy, but in a really sweet, homey way.

Everywhere I looked there were lovely things. Tiny paintings, bright cushions with bits of mirror sewn on them, shelves carved with fruit and flowers, gauzy curtains splattered with gold-painted stars, pretty crockery.

It also smelled lovely. Jewel said her mum always kept lavender oil in a special burner. "She says you can't be too careful about smells, living in a van!" Jewel filled the kettle from a little dolly-type sink.

Kenny beamed at everyone. "Don't you guys LOVE this place?"

"Where do you go to school, Jewel?" Frankie asked. She sounded as if she was interviewing her for a job or something.

Somehow I got the definite idea Frankie didn't approve of Jewel.

Jewel put the kettle on the stove. "It depends where we're living," she said. "Sometimes I don't go for months."

"Excellent," said Kenny.

"Then how will you get an education?" asked Frankie primly.

"Mum teaches me," said Jewel. "Up until I was about four, she taught art in this school in Brixton. Then she decided she'd be more use trying to save the planet." She grinned. "I know it's corny! But it's true."

I found myself smiling back. I thought Jewel was ace. But ever since we'd met Jewel, Frankie had been acting dead snooty. The truth is, Frankie likes to think she's a really unusual person. And I think Jewel made her feel, you know – ordinary.

"Do you go in for a lot of this protesting lark?" Andy asked. "You and your mum?"

"A fair bit," said Jewel. "Did you hear about that big motorway protest last year? We were there for ages. Mum actually got arrested for lying down in front of the bulldozers. They let her off with a fine, luckily."

Lyndz gasped. "Weren't you terrified she'd go to prison?"

Jewel shrugged. "Sometimes you have to stand up for what you believe in." She started taking mugs down from their hooks. "Anyone take sugar?"

Frankie gave one of her fake yawns. "Doesn't it get boring, protesting all the time?" she asked. "I mean, don't you ever do anything that's just FUN?"

"Of course she does, bird-brain," said Kenny. "She's not a protest clone."

"Of course I do, bird-brain," echoed Jewel, in a zombie voice. "I'm not a protest clone."

We all burst out laughing. Even Frankie cracked up! Jewel was a real laugh.

"So, are you guys going to tell me about this film?" Jewel asked, pretending to be fierce. "Or do I have to DRAG it out of you?"

"No, we want to tell you," giggled Lyndz. "Come on, Frankie. You're the media star."

Jewel picked up a cute little bracelet she was making. "You don't mind if I get on with this, do you?"

Jewel seemed unusually keen on bracelets. She was wearing loads, and there was a pile of them beside her.

Frankie started to explain about the school Millennium Dome and how we'd got lumbered with a zone we knew absolutely zilch about. I think Jewel was genuinely interested, because she kept interrupting to ask us questions.

She wanted to know all about the Sleepover Club. "I'd love to do that," she sighed. "But this van is WAY too titchy."

Also Jewel was dead sympathetic about our big feud with the M&Ms. In fact, everything was just buzzing along nicely when Kenny dropped a HUGE clanger.

"It'd be so-o great if you'd agree to be in our film, Jewel," she chipped in. "You'd be perfect, because you're really nice and normal. I mean, some protesters are a bit, you know..." She turned bright red.

"Sad?" Jewel suggested, a little shortly. "Weird? Hippie dippie? Happy clappy?"

Poor Kenny totally lost the plot at this point! "Phew, you're right about that stove. It's really hot in here," she said, fanning herself.

"What Kenny means," Lyndz corrected quickly, "is that other kids will be incredibly impressed to realise someone their own age can, like, care so strongly about ecology that they're willing to do something, even taking risks, to make a difference."

Are you impressed? We were totally stunned!

To everyone's relief, Lyndz's little speech really did the trick.

"OK," said Jewel calmly. "Count me in. What do you want to ask me?"

She added the finished bracelet to the pile beside her. Then she started on another one, using different colours.

Unfortunately, none of us had actually thought to prepare any questions! We stared at each other in a panic. It was *so-o* embarrassing. I mean, media people are meant to be dead cool and smooth. The Sleepover girls were really letting themselves down.

This time Frankie saved the day. "Why don't we let Jewel speak for herself?" she said sensibly. "She's the one who knows about ecology, not us!"

"OK," Jewel agreed. "If you're sure. Ready to roll, Andy?"

Andy gave her a nod. Jewel took a big breath and started talking to the camera.

"Some people think it's really weird," she said, "that people like me and Mum would actually choose to live in a van, or a tent, or even up a tree, like a wild bird or a squirrel, just to save some old field."

Jewel added that if being normal meant *not* caring about things, and shutting her eyes while people destroyed the beautiful planet she lived on, she'd rather be weird any day, thanks very much. At least that way, she'd done the best she could.

Jewel was so relaxed in front of the

camera, you'd think people popped round to her place to film her every day. Suddenly she leaned forward.

"Listen up, you kids," she said in a loud clear voice. "Nature might seem dead boring, compared to TV or computer games. But at least you HAD the chance to play hide and seek in Browses Piece. If we don't protect these beautiful wild places, one day they'll all vanish under concrete. What kind of future is that for your little brothers and sisters? So take care of Browses Piece before it's too late. OK, Cut! That's it folks," Jewel announced.

"Wow," said Lyndz. "That was excellent."

"Brilliant," said Kenny.

Frankie was blinking back tears. I think Jewel's words hit her really hard, now she's got that new little baby sister to take care of.

"Right," beamed Jewel. "Now let's think of some ways you can REALLY get one up on the M&Ms."

"*Yess!*" we all said at once.

We had a truly brilliant brainstorming

session with Jewel. For someone who doesn't go to school, she's incredibly smart. (Oh, in case you were wondering, by this time Jewel and Frankie were getting on like a house on fire.)

We were having such a great time, we completely forgot we'd left Mum out in the snow, talking to Mrs Diggins! Luckily Andy remembered, and dashed off to find her. "I want you girls to meet us by the car in ten minutes," he said.

You've probably noticed Rosie hadn't said much, since we'd hooked up with Jewel? She wasn't sulking. She was *bursting* for the loo!

She told us later she was really nervous, in case Jewel and her mum had one of those really gross chemical toilets. But finally she got so desperate she didn't care *where* she went!

Jewel quickly showed her the tiny cupboard loo. Actually, I think Jewel guessed what the problem was, because she said, "It shouldn't be TOO bad, Rosie. Mum only emptied it the other day."

"Can I ask you something personal?" I said, while we waited for Rosie to come out of the cupboard. Jewel nodded. "Why do you need so many bracelets?"

"The friendship bracelets?" said Jewel. "Oh, I sell them. That way I don't have to ask Mum for money every time I want a Twix," she grinned.

"They're cute," said Lyndz.

Frankie fingered one. It was mostly silver, with a lavender blue and minty green pattern running through it. Frankie's favourite colours.

"Would you like that one?" Jewel asked her. "It matches your jacket."

Frankie blushed. "You're giving me a friendship bracelet?"

"Of course, man," said Jewel, laughing. "I want you all to have one."

When Rosie came out of the loo, Jewel told her she was forbidden to leave until she'd chosen a bracelet.

Rosie's face lit up. "Oh, coo-ell!"

I chose a pink one, surprise, surprise. SIX

different shades to be accurate, from zingy shocking pink to pale pale rose.

After we'd chosen them, Jewel personally tied the bracelets on our wrists. "Now you're all my friends. And you can't ever take them off," she teased. "Not even in the bath."

"You ARE kidding," said Kenny.

But actually, I don't think she was.

Jewel insisted on coming with us, to make sure we didn't get lost on the way to the car. But when we got there, she gave a little business-like wave. "I'm not big on goodbyes," she said. "Love and Peace, you guys."

And she kind of melted back into the dark.

I twisted my bracelet on my wrist. Jewel and her mum were really hard up, but she'd given us these brilliant presents. Not to mention saving our skins from Mrs Cruella DeVil Weaver!!

I wish I had something to give Jewel, I thought.

But I didn't have time to feel bad, because Mum and Andy turned up. Mum had been having this big discussion with the protest women about natural beauty products!

"Some of those girls could look quite sweet," she said thoughtfully, "if they'd remember to pluck their eyebrows. Oh, Mrs Diggins says you can go round and interview her," she added.

"Excellent," said Kenny.

"Can we have this conversation at home?" complained Andy. "In case no-one's noticed, I *still* haven't had my tea."

I looked at my watch. It was only half-past eight.

I couldn't believe it! We'd had a Siberian picnic, been to our first serious protest, made a cool new friend, totally solved the problem of what to do for our project, and still had OODLES of time left for our special year 2000 sleepover!!

CHAPTER EIGHT

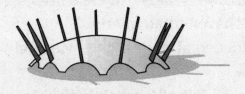

The minute we got back home, Mum insisted we'd all got to have hot baths, like IMMEDIATELY!

"I don't want anyone getting a chill," she wittered.

Phew! My fusspot mother was back to normal.

We tossed a coin to see who was going first. It was Kenny.

"Hey!" said Kenny. "I never bathed in a whirlpool bath before."

"Keep it short, Kenz," moaned Frankie.

"Don't practise your underwater breathing, OK? Otherwise we'll never get round to the actual sleepover."

"Time me," grinned Kenny. "Catch!" She tossed Frankie the sporty watch she got for Christmas. "It's got a stopwatch function," she explained. "Neat, eh?"

She skipped upstairs, humming some hippie dippie protest chant under her breath.

"Has Kenny's watch got a dynamite function as well?" giggled Rosie.

"I wish," sighed Frankie. "Ten minutes, Laura McKenzie!" she bellowed up the stairs. "Ten minutes, TOPS!"

"Or the watch gets it!!" called Lyndz in a gangster voice.

"Would you girls like a late-night snack?" Mum yelled from the kitchen.

Can you believe we were all starving? All that trudging about in the snow must totally burn up the calories! Mum promised to make us some cheese toasties after she'd made Andy his tea.

I helped the others carry their stuff upstairs. I was so-o pleased to see my room, I can't tell you. It felt really peaceful and welcoming. And after Jewel's cluttered little home it seemed absolutely HUGE!

I threw myself on my bed, practically hugging it, and sighed with pure relief.

"Jewel's van is amazing," I said. "But I wouldn't like to live in one, would you?"

"I wouldn't *mind*," Rosie said. "If my van had, you know, NORMAL facilities."

Aren't you glad it was Rosie, not Kenny who had the Protest Loo experience? I just know Kenny would have insisted in going into gruesome details, don't you!!

I don't want you to think Rosie was being horrible about Jewel's home. Actually, she said her trip to their chemical toilet gave her serious respect for Jewel and her mum.

"To tell the truth, I'm ashamed of myself," she sighed. "Meeting Jewel made me realise that I'm a totally shallow person."

"You are not!" said Lyndz.

"I am. If I had to choose between saving

a wood or a field or something, and having a bathroom, I'd choose the bathroom every time," Rosie confessed.

"I'm shallow too," I said in a small voice.

Because the truth is, if it was up to me personally to save them, all those wild, beautiful places Jewel talked about would be concreted over by now.

I'm serious.

"Maybe you wouldn't do it to save a field, but you'd do what Jewel and her mum are doing to save a person you cared about, wouldn't you?" Lyndz argued.

We stared at her. "You're right," said Rosie, amazed. "I'd do anything to save Mum and Tiff and Adam."

"So would I," I said. "I mean, for MY family. Not that I don't like yours, Rosie," I added hastily.

Then of course Frankie had to go right over the top! "If it was the only way I could save our baby, I'd live up a tree forever," she cried.

The thought of Frankie living up a tree sent us into hysterics!

"All the birds would build nests in your hair," Rosie giggled (Frankie has masses of really wild tangly hair!).

At that exact moment, Kenny's watch started making chirping birdy sounds. We *totally* cracked up.

Frankie dashed across the landing to hammer on the bathroom door.

About ten seconds later, Kenny marched out, all clean and shiny in blue stripy cotton pyjamas. She saluted. "Next!" she grinned.

It was a good thing we had Kenny's stopwatch. As it was, it was almost quarter to ten by the time we'd all had baths and changed into our sleepover things!

Rosie was wearing the sweetest little sleepsuit, which her big sister Tiffany got her for Christmas. Shorts and a floppy vest top, with the cutest embroidery around the hem. I was dead jealous!

We tossed a coin to see who was sleeping in my spare bed. (Having two beds is dead handy for sleepovers!) Frankie won the toss that time. She was suddenly looking really worn out.

The others busily spread out their sleeping bags on my carpet.

"Hey everyone," said Lyndz excitedly. "This is it! Sleepover 2000. Durn durn *durn*!"

"Yikes!" said Rosie. "I've got millennial butterflies, haven't you?"

"I've had them for DAYS!" I said. "You have no idea."

"Relax," yawned Frankie. "You and your mum did a great job."

I felt myself go red. "Oh, thanks," I said.

"We should DO something," said Kenny. "To celebrate."

Frankie groaned. "Is this celebrating going on all year, or something? A snow picnic and an ecological protest in the same sleepover ought to be enough for anyone!"

"I wasn't suggesting we, like, bungee-jump out of Fliss's window," Kenny said crossly. "I meant, do something people can, like, LOOK at in the future, so they'll know we were actually HERE, tonight."

"You mean, like a time capsule?" I said.

Lyndz sat bolt upright. "Fliss, that's such a COOL idea!"

My mum came in with our toasties. "Everyone happy?" she said.

Suddenly Frankie took a big breath, like she was diving underwater.

"Sorry if I was rude earlier, Mrs Sidebotham," she gabbled. "And I'm not trying to wriggle out of it, but none of us gets much sleep at our house. You know, since my little sister was born. And sometimes I – well, you know."

Look, don't tell the others, because it's not something I'm exactly proud of. But sometimes I don't know if I *like* Frankie very much. But just when I decide I really can't STAND her, that girl does something which knocks my socks off.

I didn't realise it, but apparently the whole time we were at Browses Piece, Frankie was feeling terrible about hurting Mum's feelings. I think she was dead brave to apologise in front of everyone like that, don't you?

Luckily Mum was really chilled about the whole thing.

"Rude?" she said, like the idea never even occurred to her. "Well, it's very sweet of you to apologise, Frankie, but I honestly didn't notice. So, I'll see you all tomorrow, shall I? Unless you need anything?" There was a hopeful gleam in her eye.

I shook my head. "Uh-uh," I said firmly. "Good night, Mum."

After we'd polished off our toasties, we had a mega argument about what to put in our time capsule.

Kenny said we all had to donate something especially precious.

Rosie pointed out that no-one in their right mind would want to stick their most precious possession in the ground for, like, *decades*.

"I mean, you wouldn't bury your Leicester City scarf, Kenz, would you?" she said.

"No WAY," said Kenny. She sounded shocked!

"Well, there you go," said Rosie sensibly.

Everyone looked depressed.

"So what are we going to do now?" Frankie asked. "Put in things we totally hate, or something? *That* makes sense. NOT!"

"I know," I said. "Suppose we don't write our normal sleepover diaries tonight. Suppose we write special millennium letters for our time capsule instead."

Frankie groaned. "If I have to hear that M-word one more time," she threatened.

"A letter?" said Lyndz. "Who to?"

"Whoever finds it in the future," I said. "You know, a future person."

Frankie perked up. "Hey!" she said. "We can put in one of those Polaroid photos of us that your mum took in the snow."

"I've got a better idea," grinned Kenny. "Ask Fliss's mum to take a new photo of us, in our night things. A serious Sleepover Club picture!"

Unfortunately, at the exact moment I stuck my head round the living-room door, my mum was just sitting down for the first time all day. But if she was fed up, it didn't show. Well, not much!

I explained our time-capsule plan. "Have you got a tin we can bury our stuff in?" I asked.

Mum did better than that. She dug out this sweet painted box she used to keep all her pretty things in when she was a little kid.

"Are you sure?" I said. She nodded. "Wow! Thanks! Whoever finds it will think they've found real buried treasure," I said.

Then we all faffed around in my room, trying out various poses, while Mum tried to stay awake.

Finally we got ourselves into position.

"OK, now on the count of three, everybody smile!" Mum commanded. "One, two, THREE!" And she snapped the button on Frankie's funky camera.

Honestly, it was the coolest photo *ever*. We all agreed that any future person finding it would be blown away!

Then Mum left us to write our millennium letters in private.

Kenny insisted they should remain the writer's deadly secret, until they were finally dug up. Until the *letters* were dug up, silly, not the writers!

"That way we can write what we want, without worrying what anyone else thinks," Kenny explained.

So we all crossed our hearts and promised we wouldn't peek.

Which is why I truly TRULY can't tell you what the other girls wrote in their time-capsule letters, OK?

But if you cross YOUR heart and totally promise never to snitch to anyone, I'll tell you what I put in mine. Here goes!

Dear Future Person

My name's Felicity Sidebotham and I'm a member of the Sleepover Club. Perhaps you don't have Sleepovers in your time? You should. They're a real laugh. Oh, by the way, in the photo, I'm the girl with long, really white—blonde hair, and I'm wearing the short pink nightie with the little hearts on. Pink's my absolutely favourite colour. How about you?

I don't know what else to tell you about myself. I'm really just average. For instance, I'm nowhere near as brave and caring as Jewel, who lives in a van and goes to protests all the time. But I love both my dads and my mum and my little brother, and I'd do anything to keep them safe, which I think is quite a good start, don't you?

Hope you are happy living in the future, and that there isn't too much concrete everywhere by the time you read this.

Yours faithfully,
Felicity Sidebotham

We folded our letters into tiny squares and put them into a plastic bag with our sleepover picture. That was Lyndz's idea. Then I wrote a message on a sticky label to put on the outside, which said: PLEASE DON'T OPEN THIS TIME CAPSULE UNTIL THE YEAR 2020.

I mean, 2020 is far enough into the future for *anyone*, right?

Finally we put the bag inside Mum's pretty treasure box and closed the lid.

"We'll bury it before we go home," said Kenny.

Frankie smothered a yawn. "Do you think we could have our feast quite soon? My baby sister woke us up about a zillion times last night."

Kenny rubbed her hands. "No problemo," she said wickedly.

Want to know what the others brought for our Sleepover feast? OK, here goes:

Pringles, a packet of squidgy pink pigs plus a packet of fizzy fish (I think Kenny got them from Marks), a HUGE white chocolate Toblerone (the Sleepover Club is going through a big white chocolate phase!) and a bag of dee-licious Caramel Swirls.

Suddenly I realised everyone was waiting. "Duh!" I grinned. "I only left mine downstairs."

I went downstairs to get my contribution. Mum helped me make it earlier in the week. It's this cake you don't actually have to cook. You make it out of biscuit crumbs mixed with other scrummy things, and it kind of firms up in the fridge. Lemon squeezy or what!

I think the others were dead touched when they saw the trouble I'd gone to. Not so much the cake, but the special topping. Because right across the cake in wobbly icing was my personal message to everyone.

welcome to sleepover 2000

After everyone had admired the cake, we switched out the light so we could have our feast by torchlight. Usually this is our favourite part of the sleepover.

But tonight we couldn't actually eat that much. I mean, if you think about it, we'd been stuffing our faces since we got back from school!! Also, we'd had a really long and exciting day, so by this time we were all having incredible trouble keeping awake.

Poor Frankie kept dozing off. But you know Frankie. She hates to miss a thing! Every now and then, she kind of peeled back her eyelids and mumbled, "What did you just say?" in a really cranky voice!

After a bit of an argument, we decided to

cut the feast short. One by one we switched off our torches. Rosie's went off last.

"Bliss!" sighed Lyndz. "I *lurve* Rosie. She finally switched on the dark."

"You are so-o silly," giggled Rosie from her sleeping bag.

"Night everyone," said Kenny.

"Night, John Boy," joked Lyndz.

There was complete silence, except for the sound of breathing.

Suddenly the phone rang downstairs. Andy answered it. "Sure, I'll tell her," I heard him say. He sounded tickled pink. "Is Frankie awake up there, girls?" he yelled.

"Mmn," mumbled Frankie. "Worra worra. Mmmn."

"Well, kind of!" I giggled.

"Her mum says to tell her they got her message. They drew the baby's name out of the hat, and it's Frankie's choice, OK!"

You should have heard us scream! I wouldn't be surprised if all Mrs Watson-Wade's curlers fell out!!!

Naturally I had to put the light back on, so

we could congratulate Frankie properly.

"OK, put us out of our misery," said Kenny, after the noise had died down. "Tell us this mysterious name!"

We were all blinking at Frankie in the lamplight. The others looked like little squinty owls, so probably I did as well!

Frankie couldn't even OPEN her eyes, but she had a big smile on her face. "Remember the name I gave that doll just before Christmas? Isobel," she murmured dreamily. "Izzy for short."

"Hey," said Lyndz. "That is so-o cool! Frankie and Izzy!"

"Ace," agreed Rosie.

"Wicked," said Kenny.

"That's such a sweet name," I said. I meant it too.

Was that a result or what? But the Sleepover 2000 fun's not nearly over yet. (Heh heh heh!) Wait till I tell you what happened NEXT!

CHAPTER NINE

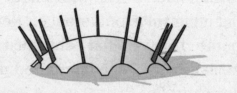

Oops! I am a TOTAL butterfly-brain. I told you all about how we came to be lumbered with the Ecology Zone, but I completely forgot to mention one TINY complication.

Unlike the actual Millennium Dome at Greenwich, ours was strictly a one-day-only event. This meant that, assuming Mrs Weaver approved of our ideas, we only had FIVE days to get the whole thing organised!!!

For various reasons, no-one in the Sleepover Club had registered this important fact until the weekend was nearly over.

I mean, before Friday, we knew diddley-dot about ecology, right? Up to then, our biggest worry was having to face Mrs Weaver on Monday and admit we'd let her down. AGAIN.

But now, thanks to Jewel's excellent input, we had a Five Star Super-de-Luxe surefire winner of a plan.

Unfortunately, we had next to no time to carry it out!! Plus, just to make things that little bit harder, we'd got to keep the M&Ms completely in the dark about our activities!

Why? Perleaze! Here are just three of the many, *many* reasons:

1. The M&Ms never miss an opportunity to get even. If they guessed we were up to something, they'd do ANYTHING to sabotage us.

2. The M&Ms are already into themselves in a really big way. If they suspected we were deliberately trying to get one up on them, they'd see it as a HUGE compliment.

3. In other words, we wanted to totally FLATTEN the spiteful little toads, but look dead cool and casual at the same time!!

"It's got to be an undercover operation, OK?" said Kenny.

This was on Sunday evening. It was the fifth time she'd phoned that day, to tell me what Frankie had just rung to tell *her*!

"We've got to lull the M&Ms into a false sense of security," Kenny went on. "We want them to think we're totally out of our depth. Whimpering into our pillows..."

"Dribbling into our stew," I giggled.

"Then on the big day..." Kenny did her sinister chuckle. "We'll BLOW their prissy socks off!"

The minute Kenny put the phone down, I called Lyndz, so *she* could pass Kenny's message on to Rosie!

You'd think Mum would be pleased we were saving her money, instead of selfishly running up astronomically huge bills, like some other children we could mention. (Rosie's big sister Tiffany for one.) Instead Mum actually yelled at me for hogging the phone, when I was only making one FIFTH of the calls I could have made!

My final chat of the day with Kenny went
something like this:

KENNY: Fliss, promise you'll get to school by
eight at the latest.

ME: Kenz, you ARE kidding.

KENNY: I've been racking my brains and
this is our only chance. *(Whisper
whisper whisper!!!)*

ME: (incredibly impressed) You little
minx!

Now here's MY last call to Lyndz:

ME: Kenny says we've got to be at school
by eight tomorrow.

LYNDZ: Hic. Sorry, Fliss. I totally missed that
because of my hiccups! I thought, hic,
you said—

ME: I did. Be in the playground at eight
sharp. Kenny's got a totally outrageous
plan. *(Whisper whisper whisper.)*

LYNDZ: (stunned) That girl is so smart she's,
hic, scary!

MUM: Fliss, will you get off that phone! Jilly's promised to call from the States, to say if she can make our wedding.

ME: Uh-oh. Mum's in a real razz. Gotta go. See ya!

As I was trying to get to sleep, I thought of a new worry. What if it snowed really heavily and Cuddington Primary School didn't even open for business?

But when I woke up, there had actually been a slight thaw. Normally I hate it when the snow gets that gruesome Slush Puppy look, don't you? But this morning I could have stood on a chair and sung a happy little Slush Puppy song!

I was so nervous about letting the others down, that I arrived in the playground at 7.99am precisely. And guess what? The others didn't turn up. I had to stand around in the slush by myself for AGES, like a totally sad person. Kenny didn't show till ten past, and it was her idea!

The others rolled up, like, *seconds* before our headmistress drove through the gate.

We all went madly slipping and slithering across the playground, frantic to catch Mrs Poole before Mrs Weaver arrived.

Look, I'm going to fast forward this bit, OK? The actual conversation in the head's office took AGES. All you need to know is that by the end of it:

1. We convinced Mrs Poole to let us dedicate our Ecology Zone to Browses Piece. (Yippee!)

2. Mrs Poole said we could miss lessons ALL week (not counting maths), to help us get our zone finished by Saturday!

3. She agreed with us that our zone would have more impact if we kept its contents deadly secret till the last minute!! "I'll have a word with Mrs Weaver," she said. (*Yess!*)

4. Mrs Poole was so impressed to hear we'd visited the protest camp in our free time, she practically kissed us. "I had no idea you girls were so concerned about the environment," she gushed.

You did remember about us parking next to Mrs Poole's car at Browses Piece, didn't you? So did Kenny. Heh heh heh! That's what gave her the awesome idea of persuading Mrs Poole to work on Mrs Weaver for us. (Frankie thinks Kenny should be a politician when she grows up.)

Anyway, when we finally got out of our headmistress's office, Kenny collapsed in complete hysterics.

"Spaceman, you went totally too far then," she gasped, wiping her eyes. "When you spouted that stuff about 'think globally, act locally', I thought I was going to wet myself."

"It worked, didn't it?" grinned Frankie. "Mrs Poole loved it."

"She ADORES us," said Rosie.

"She was putty in our hands," sang Lyndz.

"Of course," I giggled. "We're the coolest girls in the school!"

Kenny checked her watch. "We've got exactly ten minutes. I reckon that gives us just enough time to track down Dishy Dave."

Our caretaker's real name is Mr Coleman,

but all us lot call him Dishy Dave. Apart from being unusually young and good-looking for a school caretaker, he's a brilliant person to have on your side! Honestly, that man can do just about ANYTHING!

After our useful chat with Dave, we had to go and face Mrs Weaver. Our teacher has a really suspicious mind. Do you know what she said when we told her our plans? She said, "Hmmn. This is all a bit sudden. Ten minutes in a protest camp and you're all born-again eco-warriors!"

As the others probably told you, Mrs Weaver isn't *nearly* such a soft touch as our head. However, since Mrs Poole was rooting for us, Mrs Weaver couldn't exactly make a fuss. About us getting off lessons, I mean. But boy, did that woman come down hard on us in maths!

It was worth it though. We were having *excellent* fun with the M&Ms and their loyal poodles, Alana and Regina.

You wouldn't believe how easy it is to lead the M&Ms up the garden path. Those girls are so in love with themselves, they truly believe everyone else is a total dimwit.

All we had to do was let them accidentally 'overhear' our private conversation in the girls' toilets!

You've got to picture us washing our hands *incredibly* slowly, OK? And behind a row of locked doors, the M&Ms, plus Alana and Regina, were all silently earwigging like crazy.

"I wish I'd never heard of ecology, don't you, Frankie?" said Kenny, winking at Frankie.

"Totally, Kenny," agreed Frankie, sounding stressed out. "Izzy still wakes us a billion times a night. I'm really having trouble coping with this project on top of having a new baby sister." She nudged me.

"I just had no idea ecology would be so hard," I whined, making my voice weedier and more gerbil-like than usual. Then I pulled a face at Lyndz.

Lyndz sighed dramatically. "It IS a mega responsibility, Fliss. Still, it's too late to wriggle out of it. We've just got to do the best we can."

Rosie gave an Oscar-winning sob. "Face it, you guys. Even with all the extra time Mrs Poole gave us, there's no way we'll pull this thing together by Saturday. It's going to be a disaster."

And we shuffled away in a deeply tragic manner!!

At dinner time, the M&Ms kept darting really cocky looks in our direction. It was totally obvious they were talking about us.

"Heh heh heh. I think we got a result, guys," chortled Kenny.

By the way, I don't know about the others, but I wasn't totally putting it on earlier. I really WAS worried the Sleepover Club had bitten off more than it could chew! We'd given ourselves an absolutely outrageous amount to do in a ridiculously short time.

I don't think I've ever worked so hard in my life as I did in that poky stockroom Mrs Poole was letting us use for a base.

On Wednesday afternoon, Dishy Dave tapped on the stockroom door. He looked dead pleased with himself. "Come and tell me what you think," he said.

We followed him into the hall.

"*Coo-ell!*" said Kenny.

"The wood's pretty rough. I found it in a skip." Dave grinned and tapped the side of his nose. "But you can't really see it behind the curtains."

Lyndz's mum had donated the curtains. They were made of dark green velvet and were incredibly long. As well as hanging them from the sides of his structure, Dave had draped some over the top as well.

It reminded me of those cute little dens I made when I was little. Remember them? The kind where you sling a blanket over two chairs and crawl inside and play house! (Only obviously Dave's creation was heaps bigger and more impressive than that.) We swished back a corner of the curtain and tiptoed into a shadowy green cave.

"Magic!" we gasped.

"The green makes it look like moss," breathed Lyndz.

"It's *perfect*," said Rosie. "Thanks, Dave!"

"And when you've fixed up all those little lights, Dave," said Frankie cunningly, "it'll be even *more* perfect."

"Give me a chance," complained Dave. "What did your last slave die of?"

Frankie beamed. "Admiration?" she suggested.

We had one last problem. Somehow we had to smuggle in the entire contents of our zone, without the other kids seeing.

In the end, Mrs Poole agreed to let us to stay on after school on Friday, even though this meant she had to work late herself.

Dishy Dave volunteered to help. "To speed things along a bit," he said.

Can you believe that even with us all working flat out, our Ecology Zone wasn't finished till 7.30pm on Friday night?!

Finally Kenny slumped to the floor. "I'm so shattered I can't tell if it's OK, or just total rubbish," she whimpered.

"Me neither," yawned Lyndz.

Dave gazed around one last time before he pulled the curtains shut and firmly safety-pinned them together, to discourage any unofficial peeking.

He shook his head. "No, it's OK," he said. "Definitely OK."

CHAPTER TEN

OK, big apology coming up. No, I'm serious. I'd be going completely ballistic if I was you. I'd be thinking, when IS that little fluff-brain going to get to the point? You're DYING to know what was keeping us girls so busy in the stockroom, aren't you? (Heh heh heh. So was Mrs Weaver.)

I'm *truuuly* sorry I had to keep you in the dark so long, but hang on to your hat. Durn durn DURN. Get ready for me to tell you all about the Sleepover Club's finest moment!!

All I've got to do is press REWIND and take

you whizzing back to that January day when Cuddington Primary School had its very own funky Millennium Dome...

Hope you don't hate crowds, because our school hall was totally BUZZING that day. We didn't need to worry about any unscheduled peeking. Everyone was too busy sorting out last-minute technical hitches of their own! Somehow we'd kind of forgotten that our Ecology Zone was just one part of a major school event.

Miss Platt's class did a Storyteller Zone. We'd never seen a real live storyteller before, so we thought we'd pop down and earwig for a bit. She was quite an eyeful – draped in a blue velvet robe covered with appliquéd stars and moons. She'd brought this kind of clothes-airer with her, bristling with weird rattles and shakers. Whenever she needed a sound effect, she'd whip something off the airer. All the mums and dads were mesmerised by her. We were mostly fascinated by her hair. You could have used it to stop traffic!

Lyndz bought a bag of Indian sweets in the Nourishment Zone, which she said reached absolutely COSMIC levels of deliciousness. Well, that's what she said after the first three. After a couple more she went a bit quiet!

I think being a big sister has really changed Frankie, because she went incredibly soppy about some infants she saw making Chuck Wagon Stew with Mrs Carpenter.

"OK, to you and me, it's just a pan of baked beans with cocktail sausages mixed in," she burbled. "But those little kids were totally convinced they were cooking real cowboy food!"

Personally, I was still recovering from wandering into the Body Zone by mistake, and coming face to face with this, like, gigantic papier mâché model brain. I had no IDEA brains looked like the insides of walnuts, did you? It was so gruesome (and so GREY), my knees went completely to jelly.

Kenny heard me kind of moaning to myself. So she rushed over to see what was up. But instead of giving me some sympathy, she went into this major scientific rapture. "I'd just LURVE to have one of those in my bedroom," she gushed. "Hey! I could use it for a lamp."

Can you believe that girl!

I told her I don't even want to THINK about what my brain looks like, thank you very much. This sent the others into shrieks of laughter for some reason.

Oops, I nearly forgot to tell you about our really cool ecology outfits. (That's most unlike me!!) We'd decided it would be loads more impressive if we dressed the same. Identical white T-shirts, blue denim jeans and trainers. Guess who suggested printing funky Eco messages on the T-shirts? *Moi,* naturally!

We put THINK GLOBALLY – ACT LOCALLY across the front, because that's become like our personal Eco motto. You'll see why in a minute.

We were going to try to make ourselves look like real eco-warriors. But Kenny worried that it would look like we were taking the mick. There was also this TINY body-piercing problem! Plus, with the Sleepover Club's rather sad dependency on flush toilets and hair conditioner, it seemed a bit dishonest to pass ourselves off as hard-core protesters.

On the other hand, we wanted to show that even if we WERE softies, we were still totally on the side of, you know, Nature.

Eventually Rosie came up with the cute idea of painting little flowers on our cheeks. Mine are daisies. Hope they're not TOO wonky. Lyndz did them. And I don't have to tell you what happened to her right in the middle, do I? That's right. A MAJOR attack of the H-word!!

Did you notice I've been avoiding mentioning a certain Zone? Well, as it turned out, the Media Zone was actually OK. I think I'd maybe give it – six out of ten?

Regina Hill made an excellent silent movie star. Actually, if she didn't hang around with the M&Ms, I'd probably think she was cool!

She was supposed to be some actress called Mary Pickford. (No, I hadn't heard of her either. But she must have worn oodles of eye make-up!) But I can't say I was impressed with boring old Alana Banana as Charlie Chaplin (though she does have rather bandy legs! *Miaow!*).

Being silent movie stars, Alana and Regina weren't supposed to talk. Instead they held up cards with silent movie captions on, like: "Untie me! I hear the train coming down the track!" I think that's such a wicked idea, don't you?

But in all truthfulness (and I'm not being horrible here), we really couldn't tell WHO the M&Ms were meant to be. In the end we had to ask. Would you believe, Laurel and Hardy?

Kenny fell about when we told her. "Those two are such little stick insects, they look more like Laurel and Laurel!" she cackled.

Personally, I thought we could afford to ease up on the M&Ms for an hour or two. You see, even though no teachers gave us ANY help with our zone whatsoever, just about everyone who saw it was *madly* impressed. In fact, I heard one lady say our work was in a totally different league!

So we'd won, hadn't we? Game, set and match! Poor old Laurel and Laurel were practically spitting with envy.

Tell you what. Why don't I give you your very own private tour round our Ecology Zone? I'm serious. You can be our star guest!

Just shut your eyes and duck under the velvet curtain.

Now open your eyes again. Aaah, isn't it the loveliest thing?

Do you like those twinkly stars and planets hanging from the ceiling? Rosie and Lyndz did them. And don't you LURVE how we divided up the space into smaller areas inside? Oops, don't peek at the others yet! The first one is meant to represent the desert, right? Sand, cacti, that kind of thing. I think we went a bit overboard with the house plants in the jungle bit. I mean, OK, a jungle is meant to be, like, bursting with plants, but this is ridiculous!

It took forever to make those blossoms. They look dead real though, don't they? The frog sounds and monkey calls were my idea. Atmospheric or what! Andy's such a sweetheart. He taped loads of jungle sounds for us, off one of his wildlife videos.

The next bit gave us a BIG headache. In case you wondered, it's meant to be the ocean. Oh, you guessed. Coo-ell. So it really works!

The big problem with oceans is that in real life they never ever stop moving. This means you can't, like, fill a dish from the tap and just pretend it's the sea. We tried and it looked totally naff. Lyndz suggested having a tank with live fish swimming around, but as I pointed out, you can see one of those at our dentist's.

We were totally tearing our hair out, when Rosie saved the day. She was channel-hopping at home when she caught this Chinese dance group. And guess what? They were creating an absolutely *wicked* ocean, with just a few shimmery chiffon scarves! Rosie was so impressed, she rang us all up at about ten o'clock at night to tell us all about it!

Then Dishy Dave suggested using an electric fan to get the proper billowy effect. The transparent fish were Frankie's idea. And what with Dave's cunning lighting and all those pebbles and shells, I think it really suggests that lonely sea-shore feeling, don't you?

If you listen hard, you can hear some of Andy's environmental sounds. No, it isn't foghorns, bird-brain. And it's not his tummy rumbles either! It's dolphins and whispery ocean waves.

Look, I'm not going to make some big hairy deal about this next part, because the fact is, you either get it or you don't. It's an exhibition, OK?

We call it: SAVING BROWSES PIECE.

One or two of the people we showed around didn't get it at all. It was like they simply couldn't understand why a bunch of kids picked some stupid meadow hardly anyone knows about to be the most important part of their Ecology Zone.

"What about the dolphins?" these clever

people said in their snooty flutey voices. "What about the tigers? I mean, what about the OZONE layer, darlings?"

We didn't bother to argue. We just went into silent movie-star mode and pointed politely to our T-shirts.

And they'd say, "Oh. Act Locally. Oh. I see. Oh."

Anyway, let's forget about them. Much better watch Jewel instead.

This is her on the monitor. "... to save some old fields," she's saying. Mrs Diggins comes on right after Jewel says: "At least that way I know I've done the best I can."

Andy fixed it so our Browses Piece film plays continuously. I know it practically by heart now. In a minute, poor Mrs Diggins gets dead emotional. It's when she looks at the photo of her and Mr Diggins in their courting days. The picture is ever so creased and faded. But you can still tell where it's meant to be, which is the main thing.

I'll talk you through the rest of our exhibition, OK?

We found the wild flowers in garden and country-life magazines. Then we cut them out and blew them up on the school's colour photocopier. We wanted the daisies and buttercups giant-sized, just like when Frankie was a baby toddling in a daisy and buttercup forest! I decided they should SMELL right, too. So I sprayed the entire area with Meadow Sweet air freshener for AGES. Then the others pointed out to me that this probably wasn't very ecological!

Do you remember that picture our headmistress showed us in assembly that time? The old-fashioned picnic one that started this whole business off? Well, we got Mrs Poole to let us have a copy.

Frankie carefully sliced out all the original villagers, those poker-faced looking men and women and stern little babies. Then she cleverly glued them onto a new, really hideous background.

Instead of their beautiful flowery meadow, she stuck them in front of a gigantic colour blow-up of a DIY hypermarket! Sinister or what!

Frankie thought up a wicked caption too:

Spot the deliberate mistake!

The Leicester Mercury people were so impressed, they used her poster in this big feature they ran about the protest.

Oh, didn't I tell you about that? Frankie was over the moon. Plus, when the Mercury did the write-up of the school Millennium Dome, our zone was the ONLY one to get a special mention!!

They also used this ace quote from Kenny, which she absolutely denies saying. About how when it comes to saving the planet, some children don't believe they can make a difference, but they totally can!!

And even if Kenny didn't actually say it, it's still true. I mean. Mrs Poole told us it was that article in the Mercury which finally persuaded the council to save Browses Piece after all!

Not only that, but thanks to us, our village came up with the PERFECT way to celebrate the new millennium.

Yikes!! I've been so busy nattering, I forgot to keep an eye on my watch.

Oh-oh. See that coach pulling out of the school playground? Well, I'm supposed to be on it! I can't believe this is happening. Hey – wait for me! I SAID, WAIT FOR ME!!!

CHAPTER ELEVEN

Phew! I'm still getting my breath back, aren't you?! Can you believe Kenny and the others had to scream blue murder until the driver finally agreed to stop and pick me up!! Mrs Weaver was NOT amused.

It's all right for her. If it wasn't for having totally brilliant mates, I'd have completely missed the chance to take my place in History, like Mrs Poole said.

Originally we were going with our families. But the school laid on this coach, and we thought it would be more of a laugh to go together.

Didn't I tell you where we're going? OK, you remember that new village photograph Mrs Poole was talking about, to celebrate the year 2000?

Well, thanks to the outrageous brilliance of You Know Who, the parish council changed their minds about using our school as the venue. Can you guess where they want it taken instead?

Yesss! Browses Piece!! I think those old-style villagers would be really pleased we were keeping up their tradition, don't you?

As you might guess, hanging around the countryside in the freezing cold while some photographer tries to get the entire village population to face in the same direction isn't NORMALLY our idea of fun.

But in the circumstances, we wouldn't miss it for the world. Nor would Mr and Mrs Diggins.

Did I mention that Andy took us back to the protest site a couple of days ago? We'd clubbed together to buy Jewel a little thank-you present. Nothing major. Just some embroidery silks. She must get through tons making those little bracelets.

But the camp was deserted. Jewel and her mum must have moved on, to protest somewhere else.

Maybe she saw us in the paper. I hope she did.

Hey, we're there! I'll have to beetle off to join the others in a minute.

But before I go, I'll let you in on a little private joke.

Hang around a bit, and watch for that moment when the photographer finally gets us all lined up and tells us to yell "Cheese".

Want to know what we've decided to yell instead?

Sure you do! All together on a count of three. One, two, three..

"MILLENNIUM!!!"

Have a great century. Love and Peace. Bye!